Elisabeth and the Water-Troll

❀ ❀ ❀

Other Books by Walter Wangerin, Jr.

The Book of Sorrows

The Book of the Dun Cow

In the Beginning...There Was No Sky

Potter, Come Fly to the First of the Earth

Thistle

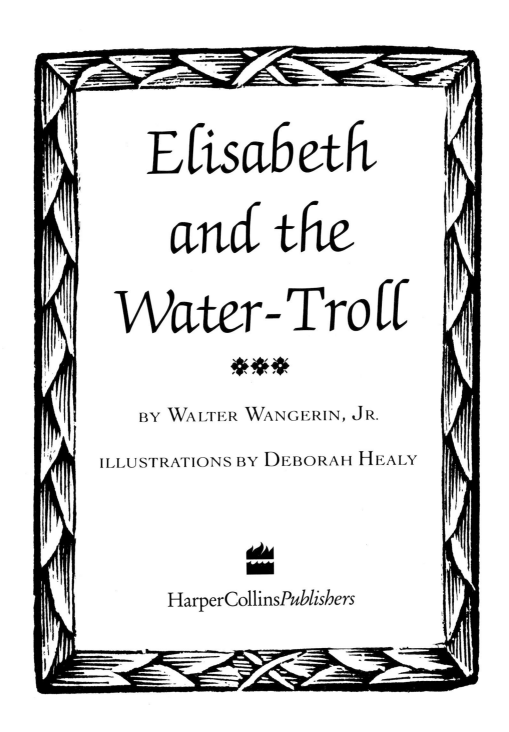

Elisabeth and the Water-Troll

❊ ❊ ❊

BY WALTER WANGERIN, JR.

ILLUSTRATIONS BY DEBORAH HEALY

HarperCollins*Publishers*

Library of Congress Cataloging-in-Publication Data
Wangerin, Walter.
   Elisabeth and the water-troll / by Walter Wangerin ; illustrations
by Deborah Healy.
      p.   cm.
   Summary: A motherless girl rediscovers hope and love when a
lonely, misunderstood water-troll takes her down into his well.
   ISBN 0-06-026353-9. — ISBN 0-06-026354-7 (lib. bdg.)
   [1. Trolls—Fiction.] I. Healy, Deborah, ill. II. Title.
PZ7.W1814El   1991   90-4359
[Fic]—dc20   CIP
                                        AC

Elisabeth
and the
Water-Troll

❀❀❀

Prologue:
The Well, The Troll, Elisabeth

❈ ❈ ❈

AN ANCIENT PATH goes north from the village of Dorf. It cuts through the woods and fields, drops down into a valley, then winds across the valley floor until it ends at a well. The villagers know this well. They call it Despair.

It's an old, old well—older than any remember, and cold because its shaft goes deep, and still. The stones that surround it are green, all covered with moss. Lizards slip between the cracks. Lizards peep out with leatherlike stares and vanish when the wind grows sharp—for the wind at the well grows sharp indeed. Down the length of the valley the wind will cry, *Beware, beware!* In the well itself the wind will whisper, *'Tis bitter, this water, and chill.*

Nobody comes here—or nobody nearly. The women who wash with water don't come, nor the men who drink, nor the children who play from morning to night. Not even the dogs of the village will creep by the Well Despair, because they know. Everyone knows. They've heard the stories by firelight, and all of the villagers know—that there dwells within the well a Troll.

Ah, the Troll, the very reason why the well is called Despair! What shall we say of him? What is the truth and not a lie?

Well, he isn't a mole, because he's too much like a

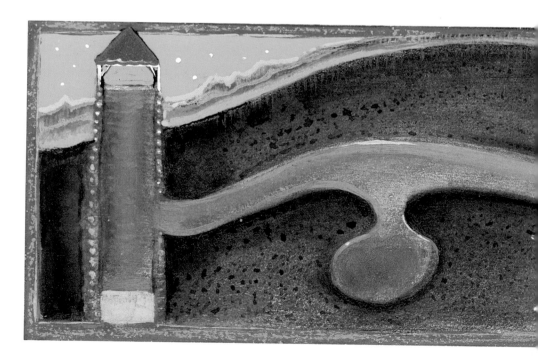

man. He frowns like a man. Yet he can't be a man exactly, because he digs in the darkness and shrinks from the light. His arms are long and powerful. He has claws on his fingers and fangs in his mouth and green in his eyes, and he leaps from the ledges inside his well as lightly as a cat. His fur is thick; his back is hunched; his whiskers are wet—and always his brow is frowning since always he's trying to think, and thinking is hard for the Troll, who isn't a man exactly.

Nobody comes to the well. Or nobody nearly…

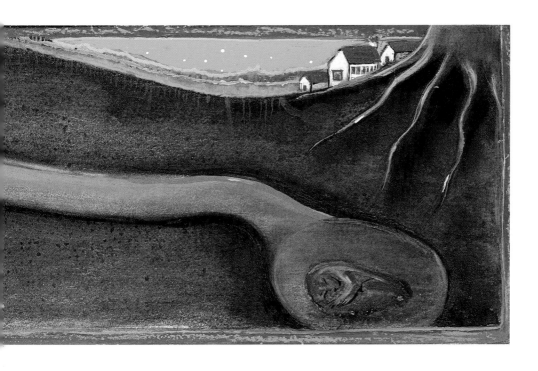

One day a small girl does come after all, and then the Troll tries harder than ever to think, because now he has something important to think about.

As if she were blind, the girl comes stumbling down the ancient path and over the valley floor. She's shaking her head. Maybe she's worried. She bumps into the stones of the well, then stops and shakes her head again and sighs. Maybe she's lost.

All at once the small girl bursts into tears.

"Ow! Ow-oo!" she cries. The Troll looks up and begins to listen.

This poor child is wailing like the wind, but she is younger and sadder than the wind, and the Troll hears the difference.

"Oh, Mama!" she wails. Like rain her tears spill down the well, but they are warmer than the rain; they sting

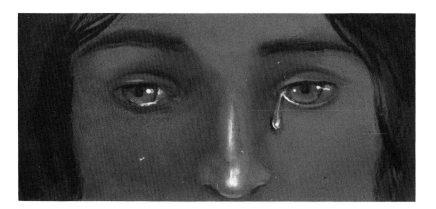

like sorrow, and the Troll can feel the difference.

"Mama!" she cries. "Oh, Mama, why did you have to die?"

To die? The Troll holds his breath. He covers his mouth and makes no sound.

"You lied to me," she cries. "You said that you loved me—but how could you love me and then go away?" She makes fists and begins to hit the stones. "You didn't love Elisabeth. You died! You said you loved me, but you left me. Mama! Mama! You lied!"

Suddenly the child puts her hands to her head and yanks from her hair two combs made out of tortoiseshell. The hair flies wild around her head. The combs she shakes above the well. "What do I want with your things?" she cries. "Papa gives me your pretty things to wear—but I won't. He tries to make me happy, but I won't be. No, I won't!" One after the other the poor girl throws the combs into the well. "Gone!" she shouts. "Gone!" Then she slumps against the stones and sobs, "No, I won't trust nobody, nobody, since everybody lies...."

So speaks Elisabeth.

And now the Troll is frowning dreadfully. He is staring at two combs he has caught, and is trying to think one good and helpful thought.

Part One:
To Dorf,
before the Dawn

❀ ❀ ❀

THERE'S A MIST in the valley in moonlight. The sun will rise and burn that mist away. But first, while people are sleeping and nobody knows it, something more monstrous is arising. The Troll is coming up.

His head and shoulders heave above the well. His eyes glow green in the night. His cat feet step on the mossy rock—then suddenly he leaps, and with a loping gallop the horrible Troll is running, running.

Across the valley floor, up the hills like a stallion he goes.

Over the fields, down empty roads, through woods, through gardens, through gates—until he comes to Dorf, where the houses are shut. The Troll is in the village of Dorf, and no one, no one knows.

He stands by the church. Three times he turns in the village square, sniffing the breezes. Suddenly he sees grey light in the eastern sky: the sun is coming and he has to hurry. Hurry, Troll!

> *One*, he's the shadow that falls on the door.
> *Two*, he's a cough in the night.
> *Three*, he is counting the houses—till *four*,
> He rears like a horse at the smell of a war—
> There! There is the house he is searching for:
> Small and wood and white.

Quietly the Troll goes creeping across the lawn. He puts his face to the window glass and peers in with old, old eyes. He sighs at what he sees. "Bonnie Lass," he growls.

Inside the room on a little pillow lies Elisabeth asleep. She is beautiful.

This Troll can move like water—anywhere, through any crack or crevice. Like water, then, he steals into her bedroom and holds his breath as he bends above the child. His heart is rushing as hard as a river.

> Elisabeth has pale white skin.
> The Troll is lifting her
> Her hair so black, her arms so thin

Hang like a broken violin.
The Troll begins to purr:

"Thee be—" he says. He swallows, unused to speaking, unused to so much feeling. "Beth, Beth," he says, "thee be my guest."

But quick! The dawn is coming!

Hurry, Troll. Begone before the sun. Begone!

In an instant the Troll has leaped from the room with the child against his breast. He's running. Faster than sunrise he goes. His hair streams in the wind, his teeth flash, the breath woofs in his chest. But the child doesn't wake because he cushions her so tenderly. Down the path like a flying stallion, down the valley, galloping, galloping toward the well—and there, in a single, magnificent motion, he springs. He sails through the air, dives down his hole, and is gone.

When the sun comes up that day, the Troll has disappeared, and the valley is as empty as it ever was. The Troll is deep underground, gazing at the child Elisabeth.

He has laid her in a lizard shell and spread her hair around her. With a rough knuckle he is brushing her cheek. And here is a wonder they never tell by firelight: he is weeping. The Troll is weeping to see this child on a ledge in the Well Despair—for her mouth is so sad, and her brow is so beautiful.

"Babe," he growls. "Baby best."

He is frowning on account of a difficult thought, how to make one sad heart happy.

"Pretty. Pretty. Prettiest."

Part Two:

Dorf, in the Morning

❖ ❖ ❖

MOST OF THE VILLAGE is still asleep, though the sun is up now, burning the mist away. Most of the people are dreaming in their beds—but not for long. They're about to be roused by a loud sound and by fear.

One man is wide awake in Dorf. He's standing in the village square wearing nothing but a nightshirt. "Eliza?" he calls. His hair is tangled. He hadn't the comb or the time to comb it. He's turning round and round, peering in shadows, searching for something.

"Eliza!" he cries as loud as he can. "Eliza Beth, where are you?"

There is no answer.

The poor man holds up two little slippers, as though these might explain his trouble. "People!" he shouts at the houses. "Has anyone seen my daughter? Does anyone know where Elisabeth's at?"

Nobody answers. Nobody's up but the sun.

So the man bows his head and hurries to the church and goes inside. He's not a young man, not a strong man, not even a straight man since his back is bent. But he knows how to pull a bell cord—

BONG!

The church bell has a deep, round throat and a tongue of iron. This bell is the crier of Dorf, when there's fire, or danger, or death—

BONG!

Who can sleep when the bell is ringing?

BONG!

Windows fly open. Heads pop out. People begin to chatter. "What's wrong? What's—"

BONG!

The Mayor stumbles from his doorway, yanking his belt above his belly. "Who?—"

BONG!

The Sheriff charges down the street, strapping a sword to his side. "Where?—"

BONG!

Men grab clubs. Women run outside. People crowd the village square. "When?—" *BONG!* "Why?—"

BONG!

"Who's tolling the dreadful bell?—"

BONG! BONG! BONG!

It's the Parson, finally—a man as long as a stick of chalk—who goes to the church and stands outside the door. "That's it! That's it!" he thunders. "Be ye flesh, or be ye Devil, come out in the daylight and show yourself! Come!"

The bell falls silent.

Immediately the Sheriff draws his sword, and the men grip clubs, and the Mayor wishes he weren't the Mayor—

But the door cracks open to reveal a little bent-backed man in nothing but a nightshirt, carrying something muddy against his chest. "Peter!" Everyone knows Peter.

"Why, it's only Peter," declares the Parson, and a wonderful change comes over the crowd. They all seem bolder.

Immediately they all grow angry too.

The Sheriff slams his sword into its scabbard. "Well, that was a rude thing to do," he snaps, "disturbing our sleep."

The people mutter, "To be sure," and "Impolite," and "Right."

And the Mayor is glad to be Mayor again, the official voice of the village. He hitches his belt and clears his throat and lifts his chin on high. "You'd better have a good reason for ringing the bell, sir," he says.

Peter whispers, "I do."

"Out with it! Out with it," says the Mayor, turning to face his citizens. "Tell us at once."

But Peter can't speak at once. He whispers the single word "Elisabeth," then hugs two muddy objects to his breast and struggles not to cry.

"Yes? Yes?" the Mayor repeats. "Elisabeth—and *what*?"

"My daughter is gone," says Peter.

"What? Your daughter is what? Speak up, man, so the people can hear you."

Suddenly Peter howls at the tops of his lungs, "Elisabeth is kidnaped!"—and immediately all of the people are a little less bold. They know trouble when they see it, and they all have children of their own. They shuffle their feet and murmur the awful word: "Kidnaped?"

The Mayor glances back and forth between the people and Peter. "Well," he says. He clears his throat. "Well, well," he stutters. Then he hitches up his belt and announces, "Well, you're probably wrong. Yes, that's it. You're wrong, sir. Elisabeth just ran away. She's hiding somewhere—"

"No!" shouts Peter. "She was kidnaped. And it's worse than that. Look," he cries to all of the people. "Look what I found in her bedroom!"

The people press closer to see what Peter is holding up: two little slippers, both of them muddy with dark green slime.

"Little girls don't run away without their slippers," Peter cries. "And there's mud in her bedroom, mud on her bed. Something muddy and ugly has stolen my daughter away. People, people, help me to find her!"

Immediately the Mayor is wishing he weren't the Mayor again. He starts to clear his throat and discovers that he can't talk for a while. The people too are deathly quiet, staring at the dark green slime. Nobody says a word.

"Will you help me?" Peter asks.

"Parson?" the people murmur. They can't take their eyes from Elisabeth's slippers. "Parson?" they ask.

"Where does green slime come from?"

In his marvelous voice the Parson answers a terrible answer: "I don't know," he says.

The worst is not to know.

Peter pleads, "But will you help me?"

"Parson?" the people repeat. "Parson, what creature drips green slime?"

The Parson says, "I don't know."

The people beg, "But will he come back tonight?"

"Well—" says the Parson.

"What?" cry the people. "You mean he might?"

"Well—" says the Parson.

"You mean he *will!*" Now no one is bold anymore. Everyone's terrified. "He will!" The whole crowd begins to babble and bellow, "And we have children of our own! Oh, what are we going to do?"

Amazingly, the Mayor has disappeared. But soon, like a cannon, one voice is booming above the others, calling and calling till all of the people are paying attention: "Follow me!"

It's the Sheriff! His sword is already drawn. "Follow me!" he roars. "I am a man of action! I know what we're going to do!"

Oh, thank God for men of action! Thank God for something to *do*!

"Follow me! We'll catch this muddy baby-snatcher, and we'll give him what he deserves. Evil given, evil gotten, right?"

"Right!" say the men, feeling much better.

"A slasher should be slashed," booms the Sheriff, "right?"

"Right!" shout the men, lifting their clubs and feeling bolder after all.

"And a killer," roars the Sheriff, "should be killed, right?"

And all of the men say, "Right!"

❊ ❊ ❊

Soon there is no one left in the village square save one man in a nightshirt, hugging two small slippers. He's talking to himself.

"Eliza, you're barefoot," he says. This seems to him an enormous sadness. "You're going to catch a cold," he says. Suddenly he raises a hand and touches his tangled hair. "And what did you do with your mother's combs?" he asks. "Where are they?"

What a silly question to be asking! But the poor man asks it anyway, because he can't bear to ask the other question, which has no answer:

Eliza, where are you?

Part Three:
The Well,
in the Afternoon
❋ ❋ ❋

ALL DAY LONG Elisabeth has been sleeping, the
sorrowful child. But day is like night in the Well
Despair. It is always dark down there.

And all day long the Troll has been busy—busier and
happier than he has ever been before. In and out of his
chambers, up and down his tunnels he has gone,
preparing, arranging, and making ready for the moment
when the child will wake.

It broke his heart to feel her tears and to know how
sad a girl could be. Therefore—

> The Troll has made Elisabeth
> A gown of grass, a glove of glass,
> A shawl of baby's breath.
> He's shod her feet in shucks of wheat;
> He's brought her buttercups to eat;
> He's carved a diamond for her seat—

and when at last she stirs, when the little girl coughs and wakes and looks around, lo: there is the Troll, smiling horribly.

> Ah, when she wakes, he saith,
> "Thee be my Queenling, Beth."

That's what the Troll says through his fangs. And he means it kindly. But to the ears of a child it sounds savage and brutal, like an animal snarling.

Elisabeth is in the home of the Troll. He considers it a comfortable place. But to the eyes of a child it's a dungeon with water dripping all around. It's dark and cold, and lizards are licking her feet. Elisabeth whimpers and starts to sit up. She's staring at the green-lit eyes of a monster who is staring back at her—a hairy monster, huge and wet. He's reaching toward her.

"Bonnie Lass," he snarls, "somebody cares for thee. Nay, somebody does not lie—"

She sees the claws coming toward her face. She tries to shrink away, but the arms are long and strong, and they keep on coming. And the forehead of this beast is twisting in a hideous frown.

So the instant one claw touches her, the poor child jumps to her feet and screams.

"Nay!" growls the Troll, frowning deeper and deeper. "Nay, I mean no harm—"

But it's harm that Elisabeth hears. She begins to stumble backward from the beast, still watching him.

"Stop!" the Troll explodes. Like thunder his voice goes echoing through the caves. He starts to rise, but this is too much for the girl. She turns and runs as fast as terror will take her.

"Danger!" bellows the Troll. "Danger, Beth! 'Tis only a ledge in front of thee—"

For a moment the girl is running on stone, then suddenly she sails into the empty air. "Papa! Papa!" she shrieks. She somersaults. Above her she glimpses a circle of sky, below her a pit of blackness, and now she is falling down—down and down the shaft of the Well Despair.

"Papa!"

The Troll doesn't frown anymore. The Troll doesn't even try to think, since thinking would take too long. He acts. He runs to the edge of the shaft and leaps.

Elisabeth, kicking and waving her arms, is sinking like a silken scarf. But the Troll has rolled himself into a ball and drops like stone, fast and faster. Soon he passes her. Then far below he flings out an arm and grabs at the wall and finds a grip. His body slams against the rock; yet with one arm he hangs on, and with the other he sweeps the air until he feels the falling child and catches her.

"Ohhh!" he groans. Their double weight has broken him. "Oh, heaven, heaven!" But he keeps the girl. He presses her against himself. And Elisabeth, she does the same, winding her fingers into his hair and clinging like a baby to his breast.

She is shivering.

For his own pain, the Troll says, "Ohhh." But for her shivering fear he whispers, "Hush, babe. Hush thee, baby best. I vow we'll climb it, and I'll lay thee on the solid ground again."

And here is a wondrous, blessed thing: Elisabeth believes him.

Slowly, slowly he stretches and starts to climb.

Elisabeth feels the hurtful flexing of his muscles, and she hears him moan with every move—but to her ear it isn't an animal sound anymore. It's deeper than that, and kinder, as though she heard a holy river running in the regions of his heart.

Little Elisabeth ceases shivering. Before they reach the ledge, she has lost all fear because she trusts the strength and the promise of the Troll, and she isn't cold because he is so warm. A piece of her is melting. She closes her eyes. She presses her cheek against his breast. She feels his hurt as though it were her own.

"Who are you?" she whispers.

Slowly, slowly he brings them to the ledge again.

Gently he lays her in the lizard shell. And then, his vow fulfilled, he falls on the stone and does not move.

Elisabeth watches him. In a little while she whispers, "Who are you? I don't even know your name." But his eyes are closed. He doesn't answer.

Silence surrounds them in the cavern. No—not silence exactly. Water is dripping. Water is running the deeps of his home. The sound of water comes from everywhere. All at once the monster draws a terrible breath and groans, and that too sounds like water, the flow of a slow and mighty river—

Ahhh. Soon in her soul the child is saying, *Ahhh. Of course.* She's remembering the stories they tell by firelight: *This is the Water-Troll!*

While she watches the suffering beast, Elisabeth's soul is flooded with understanding: this one answers the water of tears. Yes. This one listens to the talk of all waters. He rises like mist in the night. Yes, yes! He can leak through a double-locked door, he can leak into a troubled heart, he can melt a frozen heart in pity. Of course the water drips around them. This well is the source of all of the water of Dorf—and this one is the Water-Troll.

Little Elisabeth leans over the Troll and begins to cry. She is crying because of his pain—the first such tears she's wept since her mother's death turned all her tears to bitterness.

One by one the tears splash on the Water-Troll. They startle him, and his green eyes open.

"What, child?" he growls. He raises a claw. "Art thou still crying? But I wanted to dry thy tears. Ohhh, pretty Beth," he sighs. "I did not want thee sad. I wanted to tell thee, this life is lovelier than bad. I wanted to say, 'One someone loves thee, Beth, and does not lie.'" The great Troll closes his eyes and groans. "But what hath ugliness done for thee? Why, nothing but frighten thee, and what is the good of that? Begone, my Queenling," he groans. "Go home. Forgive a Troll and forget him. Go."

But the little Queenling neither leaves nor moves. Instead, she smiles. Through the rain of her tears she

smiles as though the sun were shining. And that which
happens next in the well they never tell by firelight:

"Oh, Troll," she says; and on his chest
She lays her head as if to rest.
Indeed, he is the ugliest,
But he needs comforting.
So Beth begins to sing.
For him she sings, "Alack-a-day,"
For him a pretty roundelay
To take the pain away:
"Alas, and lack the day—"

Part Four: The Village, in the Evening

❀ ❀ ❀

THE DAY IS DONE. The night is almost here. It's twilight, and this is the situation in Dorf: the people are doing nothing.

The Sheriff is sitting in the tavern glaring at his pint of ale and saying nothing. He's mad. He found no foe the whole day through. His sword cut no one. All of his promises failed. Now, that would embarrass a lesser man, but the Sheriff never gets embarrassed. He gets mad.

Oh, he hates that baby-snatcher with a deadlier hate than he did this morning, hates him so much he cannot talk.

The men are in the tavern, too, staring at their pints of ale, saying nothing. They've got nothing to say. Can't

39

boast. Can't tell each other tales of daring deeds. They did no deeds at all today—found nothing, fought nothing, learned nothing, know nothing. Ignorant! Pitiful.

Parson, what makes green slime?

Well, I don't know.

Don't know. The worst of all is not to know, for how can anyone fight against a mystery?

But the night is almost here. The chill and the dark and the fear are coming, coming.

The women have bolted their doors. They've put their babies to bed and sit like guards beside them. They saw the mud on Elisabeth's sheets. They visited Peter in daylight, to check if his story was true. It was true. And now they sit with eyes wide open in the dark. In someone's house a baby whimpers. A mother gives it

water. Then all is quiet—

The night is almost here.

The Mayor is soaking his feet in a pan of warm water, trying to soothe his nerves from a day too full of official responsibilities.

The Parson crouches in the baptistry, praying.

And Peter is stripping the sheets from his daughter's bed, to wash them in a tub of water. There comes a moment when he buries his face in the linen, and he smells the scent of his Elisabeth, and he sighs.

But then he gets down on his knees and scrubs her floor. Slow strokes, slow strokes: for he ought to clean up; but it seems as though he is washing his daughter away. Very slow, sad strokes.

So the twilight dies. So the night descends. So Peter looks up and gazes out the window. And finally he utters the question he couldn't ask before: "Liza, Liza Beth—where are you now?"

❋ ❋ ❋

All at once, throughout the whole village, a wonderful sound is heard from a wonderful source. The sound is singing. The source is water—all of the water in Dorf!

Thirty-two mugs in the tavern break into song. One is the Sheriff's. He shatters it with his sword, while men jump backward from the music. Ale is made with Dorfer water!

And the water the children drink, it sings! Mothers snatch their babies from the singing and send the glasses flying.

The Mayor's pan begins to sing.

The village pump joins in.

And the sacred water in the baptistry—

Puddles and runnels, brooks and ponds—it's everywhere! Cups and kettles and pots—a thousand voices are singing the selfsame song: *Alas*, they sing.

Alas, alack-a-day!

All of Dorf is a choir now. And all of its people are frightened—all but one.

Little, bent-backed Peter is tipping his ear to the tub where his daughter's sheets are soaking. He listens intently. And then what does he do? He grins! He claps his hands and he laughs. Why, this is a song he taught his daughter to sing! This is Elisabeth's voice. She's singing, *Alas, alack-a-day.*

Listen: her voice is huskier, lovelier, just like her mother's. And listen: she's singing significant things. A well. A shell. A glove of glass. An injured creature whom she loves, whose name is, whose name is—

"I know!" cries Peter, rushing out of doors. "Happy day! I know where Elisabeth's at!"

"What? What?" The Sheriff bursts from the tavern, mad and prepared to be madder. "Where?"

"Yes, and I know who has her, too!" laughs Peter.

The men storm into the night, snatching clubs and lighting torches. "Who?"

"Isn't it wonderful?" Peter cries. "She's near enough to bring her home tonight!"

Here comes the Mayor: "Wonderful?" The women are following: "Wonderful?" Then the whole crowd roars together: "Wonderful! Yes! The kidnaper's near enough to murder. He won't escape a second time!"

"No!" says Peter. "It's all right. He hasn't hurt the child at all."

"*He* hasn't? *Who* hasn't?" thunders the crowd. "Our children are in danger. Who?"

Now Peter himself begins to fear. Nobody's stopping to understand that his news is good news after all.

Instead, with the swollen voice of anger they bellow, "Who?"—and then they wait.

Into a sudden silence, Peter whispers: "The Troll."

The Troll! The Water-Troll!

For an instant the crowd stands still. A dismal horror makes them sweat: *The Troll in the Well Despair?*

"You see," poor Peter tries to explain, "my daughter likes—"

"AH-*HA!*" booms the Sheriff. "I knew it! I knew it!" he shouts. "The Troll is as green as a fungus! Didn't I *say* the mud was green?"

And as the Sheriff shouts, so shout the men: "We knew it! We knew it! We were only waiting to be sure!"

When the men shout back, the Sheriff grows bolder. "We've had enough!" he declares, drawing his sword to prove it. "Shrewdly we discovered the beast. Bravely we'll dispatch him. All day long we've waited in patience, but now we've had enough!"

"Remember our children," cry the men.

"God save the children!" roars the Sheriff. "Evil given, evil gotten, right?"

"Right!"

"A slasher—" the Sheriff cries.

And the whole crowd answers, "—should be slashed!"

"A killer—" the Sheriff howls.

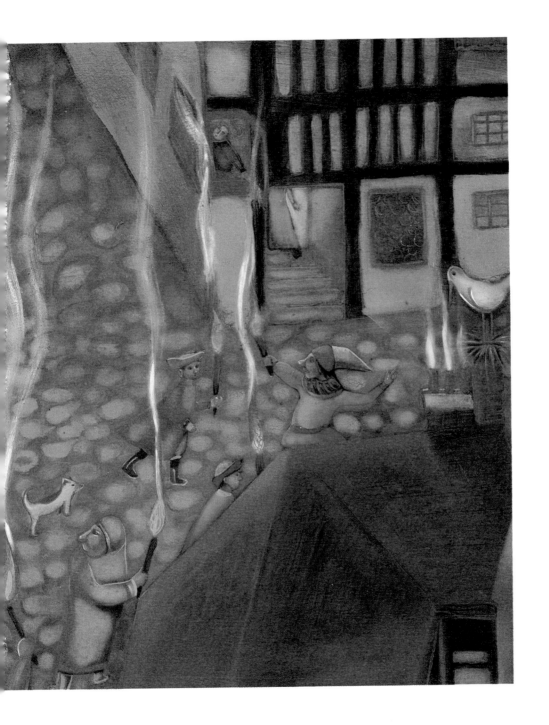

With the thrill of conviction the people thunder: "—should be killed."

And so it is, that with torches and weapons, with fire and scythes and mattocks, with rage and faith and righteousness, the people of Dorf are gone from the village. In a mob they are marching the ancient path through woods and fields to the northern valley, to the well they call Despair.

But Peter is bent in his back. He can't move as fast as fury moves these citizens. "People!" he calls as he hurries after them. "People!" he cries to the torchlight far ahead:

> "Oh, people, how I wish you heard
>   My still more gentle word:
>   Eliza isn't suffering.
>   My daughter *likes* to sing...."

Part Five:
Midnight,
the Bone-Fire,
the Ending

❊ ❊ ❊

DOWN INTO THE VALLEY sweep the people, their torches dancing. Across the valley floor they fly, their lanterns whirling, circling. They look like a swarm of burning insects. They collect at the Well Despair.

The stones of the well are not green, but red and lurid in the firelight. Tongues of torch-flame lick the black night air, and *whoosh!* goes a torch when one man whips it round his head, and *whoosh!* goes another, *whoosh!* when it is waved.

The people make a circle around the well.

"Troll!" It's the Sheriff, delighted to be mad and to be here. "Troll, come out of your hole!"

"COME OUT!" cry the people.

"You've had your day. You've done your dirty.

You've troubled our children enough! It's our turn now.
Never again will the children go to bed afraid—"

"OH, YOU *TROLL!*" the people thunder. "OH,
YOU *BEAST!*" they cry.

"Come out!" commands the Sheriff.

"COME OUT!" the people repeat, delirious.

"Come out!" shouts the Sheriff the loudest of all
because he is the leader, and now he leads by counting:
"One!" he cries, and the people fall silent. They stare at
the well. "Two!" he roars. He waits. "I'm going to say
three," he warns,

"HE'S GOING TO SAY *THREE!*" the people

shriek at the well, crouching and gripping their weapons the tighter. But the well in the middle stays empty—and before the Sheriff can count to three, here comes Peter, panting and pushing through the crowd and bothering everyone with his worries.

"Wait, wait," he is pleading. "Elisabeth's down there!"

"What?" shouts the Sheriff. And then he explodes: "Get back, you idiot!"

But Peter has run to the stones around the well. "Elisabeth!" he calls into the hole. "Elisabeth!"

"Grab that man!" The Sheriff is beside himself.

"Drag that man away from there!"

The people start to move, but Peter turns and begs them, "No! She's all right!"

The people hesitate, so the Sheriff stamps his foot and thunders, "Three! Three! One, two, *three!* Did everyone hear me? Three!"

"YES! THREE!" roar the people.

"That means we're done with talking. It's time for the fire! Forget that man and get me wood! Three means burn the monster. *Threeee!*"

Well, wood is an easy command. The people rush to action, and branches begin to fall around the well-stones, twigs and tinder, limbs and logs and bracken. Poor Peter is knocked to the side, while the pile grows high and higher with a hole in the center as black as the throat of a chimney.

Peter is on his knees. "Elisabeth!" he wails.

But nobody's listening anymore. Nobody hesitates.

"Troll!" the sheriff shrieks, and all of the people make a circle again. "Troll, behold your ending!" And *whoosh!*—he whirls his torch around his head, then *whoosh!* he throws it. It loops through the air and lands on the bracken. Instantly a flame leaps up, which races round the well to form a perfect, pointed, dancing crown.

Oh, the people clap and cheer! Their faces grow bright in firelight. Peter bows his head and weeps, but the people begin to sing: "OHHHHH!" they chant in a turning circle. "OHHHH, TROLL!"

But suddenly something is rising in the midst of the fire, and silence descends on the valley, and on the people a cold, cold horror—

The Troll is coming up.

Slowly, slowly, out of the hole, surrounded by flame, an arm and a shoulder, a head and a face, a dreadful and terrible frown. His eyes are open and piercing. Green. His cat feet step on the stones, and then he stands awhile within the wall of fire. He has a bundle against his breast, wrapped like a baby in long, damp hair. He crouches, hunch-backed. He gazes from person to person around the crowd—until his green eyes fall on Peter. And this is the truth: He sees the water on Peter's cheeks. He understands the tears. He is a Water-Troll.

Now he bows and tucks the bundle beneath his chin; and while the people gape, he begins to move through the blaze itself, walking on the burning wood.

What a hissing his passage makes! But he does not rush or stumble. The steam pours from his body. The tears run from his green, green eyes, but he does not groan.

Now, as he crosses the grass toward Peter, he is a smoking Troll. Great clouds ascend from him. And then he kneels in front of the weeping man, and gently he unwraps his hair, and there is Elisabeth, safe and pale and crying, too; and that makes three in tears.

"Canst hear me, Bonnie Lass?" the Troll growls, stroking her cheek. "Canst understand me, Beth?"

The child does not move. She's gazing at a dying Troll. She's grieving.

"Nay, Beth. Nay, don't cry," the monster murmurs.

Then all at once the Water-Troll stops his frowning and starts to smile. It is as though the most wonderful thought in the world has just occurred to him. He reaches to the hair on his head and one by one removes two objects.

"Thou gavest me a gift," he growls, smiling on the child, "that someone first gave thee. This someone never lied to thee, dear Beth. This someone never left thee when thy mother did, but he loved thee always, and always grieved with thee. Thy loss was his, thy hurt and all thy heart. Ah, don't the teardrops tell me so? Nod, Beth. Nod thy pretty head to me."

The poor child, her own tears streaming, nods for the Troll.

"Aye," growls the Troll, low and low and lovely.

"Good," he says. "And now I return the gift to its givers one and two—to thee, and to him who loves thee." The objects which the Troll is holding are tortoiseshell combs. One he winds into the black hair of Elisabeth. With the other he strokes her father's hair, and kindly he gives that comb to Peter. They are a set.

Thus the Troll has thought his thought and shall never frown again. He looks on the child with an infinite peace. And now—

He combs her hair. He kisses her.
"Thee be my Queenling, Bonnie Beth:
God save thee from this day," he saith,
Then breathes the next to his final breath,
   And hides his face in fur—
     Forever.

Epilogue: Eliza's Song, Eliza's Secret

SOMETIMES, sometimes an old man and a young woman of midnight hair walk down the ancient path to the valley near Dorf, to a well whose stones are black. They go arm in arm, and they whisper to one another of this wonder: that ugliness can be so beautiful. Then side by side they stand beside the well.

The old man has long white hair and short legs and a heavier hunch in his back. These come of age. There is a green glint in his eye. That comes of wisdom.

Sometimes they spy lizards slipping among the stones. They laugh.

And sometimes, because this well is still the source of all waters, they let down a little bucket, then draw it up again, and they drink.

But before she drinks, the woman tips her ear to the
water. She holds back her hair, and she listens. The
water whispers her the fondest of secrets, and she
smiles. For this is what she hears:

Thee be my Queenling, Beth.

Forever.

Water is forever.

> Now Lisabeth sings "Lack-a-day"
> As often as she may.
> And still she wears her glove of glass,
> So doth the gentle lass.
>
> For once a Troll did set her by
> For fear that she might have to die
> Within the flames which leaped so high
> Around his citadel.
>
> Elisabeth has learned to sigh
> The widow's lullaby—and why?
> He loved her, truth to tell.
> He loved her very well.